For my mother, Julia, whose father, James Adams, made the journey, and her mother, Julia, and the rest of the children—Kate, James, Carlyle, Pauline, Beatrice, Earl, and Courtney—who waited.

For Dick Jackson, who did both and who believed in this work.

—M.B.

For Angelina and her daddy, Michael.

Special thanks to Pam, Dawn, and Christopher.

—P.C.

Daddy went out in the snow.

Mama told him not to go. She said mail can wait.

She said a horse might be able to stand up to a strong wind and deep snow, but a man's not fit for it. Not even a mailman.

What's Mama talking about?
Daddy can do anything.
He can carry Daniel *and* me on his shoulders.
"Thomas," he called to me, "when I get back I'm going to make you the biggest snowman you ever saw."

Daniel, Ruth, and I watched Daddy ride off down the road on Lightfoot, the snowdrifts brushing the horse's belly. Daddy slung his empty mail pouch over his shoulder and headed to the post office, four miles into town.

You couldn't see the road anymore. A sea of snow rolled and sprayed the air thick with white sparkles. It covered everything.

The LONGEST WAIT

by **Marie Bradby**

illustrations by **Peter Catalanotto**

ORCHARD BOOKS   NEW YORK

Mama worried up two batches of rolls. She kneaded
the dough hard, smacked it against the table. She boiled
greens with fatback.

"When Daddy gets home, he's going to find my sled,"
I told her.

Ruth put the baby down twice for her nap.
Daniel sat by the window rocking time away.
"When Daddy comes, we're going to have a
snowball fight," I said.

But supper got cold. I pressed my face to the windowpane. Gray shadows crept across the waves of snow. What's taking him so long? I wondered. Is he ever coming back?

Then I saw a horse.
"Here comes Daddy!" I shouted.

We struggled through deep drifts of snow to help Daddy,
his clothes stiff with ice. His lips were cracked and bleeding.
And he was bent over.

I was so glad to see him.

Mama served supper. Daddy said the grace: "Thank you, Lord."

Daddy didn't look right, but he talked: "Herbert was stuck in the road in that old broken-down milk wagon," he told us. "Fooling with him, my hands and feet ached until they got numb.

"Near the station, the train had jumped the tracks. Buses couldn't get nowhere.

"They had an army of men trying to clear Duke Street near the post office. But ain't no use till this storm passes. Snow piled up to the knees of the war statue.

"Wind liked to cut me in two as I started my rounds. Took Miss Ethel her mail, and would you believe she was out shoveling her walk! I told her don't come bothering me when your arthritis acts up."

Daddy hardly touched supper.

"Play you a game of checkers," I said to cheer him up. But he said he was hot. He went to bed. And took sick.

He shook all over from fever. Talked out of his head all the night.

Mama prayed.

Daniel and Ruth fed the woodstove till the kettle started screaming.

I dozed with my army soldiers and wondered, Is Daddy going to be all right?

It was still and dark outside when I woke. Then I heard talking.

"Dreamt I got lost in the snow," Daddy moaned.

"Hush," Mama said. "You're home now, Samuel."

"The horse kept slipping and sliding, and I couldn't see where I was going."

"Hush," Mama said.

I almost wished it had never snowed.

Daddy saw the worry still in my eyes.

"Come here, Thomas," he said. "The storm's over." He hugged me and I felt the numbness and fever had melted away. "There's enough snow to race a sled from here to Washington. You can take the longest ride you ever had."

Sure enough, morning came clear as a whistle.
Daniel found the sled.

And I went out in the snow.

Orchard Books
95 Madison Avenue
New York, NY 10016

Manufactured in the United States of America
Printed by Barton Press, Inc.
Bound by Horowitz/Rae
Book design by Mina Greenstein
The text of this book is set in 14 point
Esprit Bold.
The illustrations are watercolor.

10 9 8 7 6 5 4 3 2 1

Library of Congress Cataloging-in-Publication Data
Bradby, Marie.
The longest wait / story by Marie Bradby ; pictures
by Peter Catalanotto.   p.   cm.
Summary: When Daddy rides off on his horse in a
terrible snowstorm to deliver the mail, his family
anxiously awaits his return.
ISBN 0-531-06871-4.
ISBN 0-531-08721-2 (lib. bdg.)
[1. Postal service—Letter carriers—Fiction.
2. Snow—Fiction. 3. Afro-Americans—Fiction.
4. Country life—Fiction.]   I. Catalanotto, Peter, ill.
II. Title.
PZ7.B7175Lo   1998   [E]—dc20   94-24875

DATE DUE

OCT 2 1 2003			